EATING DISORDERS

Published by Smart Apple Media
1980 Lookout Drive
North Mankato, Minnesota 56003

Photos: pages 8, 16—LifeART, Lippincott Williams & Wilkins;
page 10—Hulton-Deutsch Collection/CORBIS; pages 17, 27—
Indexstock: Omni Photo Communications, Inc. and Bonnie
Kamin; page 22—Moshe Shai/CORBIS; pages 24, 29—Tony
Duffy/Allsport

Design and Production: EvansDay Design

Library of Congress Cataloging-in-Publication Data

Vander Hook, Sue, 1949–
Eating disorders / by Sue Vander Hook
p. cm. – (Understanding illness)
Includes index.
Summary: Describes several eating disorders, including
anorexia and bulimia, their causes, and their impact on those
suffering from these problems. Includes a brief profile of
Cathy Rigby and her experience with eating disorders.
ISBN 1-58340-024-9
1. Eating disorders—Juvenile literature. 2. Anorexia nervosa—
Juvenile literature. 3. Bulimia—Juvenile literature. [1. Eat-
ing disorders. 2. Anorexia nervosa. 3. Bulimia.] I. Title. II.
Series: Understanding illness (Mankato, Minn.)

RC552.E18V3576   2000
616.85'26—dc21   99-29938

First edition

9 8 7 6 5 4 3 2 1

UNDERSTANDING ILLNESS

EATING

SUE VANDER HOOK

DISORDERS

Every day,
AROUND THE WORLD

DESIRE FOR FOOD IS A NATURAL RESPONSE

TO AN ESSENTIAL NEED. EACH MORSEL OF FOOD THAT PASSES THROUGH THE MOUTH AND INTO THE STOMACH SUPPLIES ENERGY FOR WALKING, TALKING, RUNNING, AND EVERYTHING ELSE A PERSON DOES. FOOD IS NECESSARY FOR LIFE. FOR SOME PEOPLE, THOUGH, FOOD BECOMES AN ENEMY. PSYCHOLOGICAL AND SOCIAL FACTORS CAUSE SOME PEOPLE TO INTENTIONALLY GIVE THEIR BODIES TOO MUCH FOOD OR NOT ENOUGH OF IT. WHEN A PERSON'S EATING HABITS ARE HARMFUL TO THE BODY, THE PROBLEM IS KNOWN AS AN EATING DISORDER.

PEOPLE EAT. THE

BODY VERSUS BRAIN

Eating should be fun. Interesting flavors and textures offer people many ways to fulfill their body's basic need for nourishment. Among the wide array of choices are juicy fruits, crisp vegetables, tender meats, and aromatic cheeses. Flavorful breads and pastas help provide the energy we need, and delicious sweets tantalize the tongue.

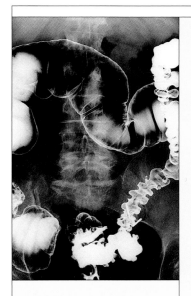

An X ray of the intestinal system. This network of tubes helps the body use digested food.

bolus: a soft, round mass of chewed food

esophagus: the tube through which food passes from the mouth to the stomach

Food is a necessary requirement for good health, but meals should also be enjoyable.

A person eats food by chewing it up into a **bolus** and swallowing it down the **esophagus** into the stomach. The food is then softened by stomach acids for about an hour. After this **digestion** has taken place, a valve at the bottom of the stomach opens up, allowing food to enter the intestines. During the digestive process, the body extracts vitamins, minerals, carbohydrates, and proteins from food. Anything left over travels to the end of the intestines, where it leaves the body.

digestion: the process of breaking food down so that the body can use it

psychological: relating to the mind

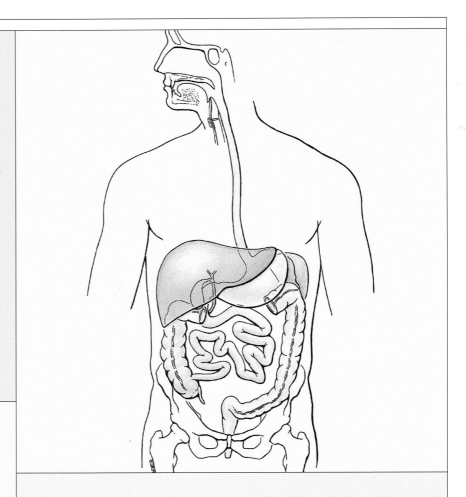

Food travels through a complex digestive system, providing nourishment for the entire body along the way.

Even though the body usually has perfect judgment regarding the amount of food it needs, complex **psychological** obstacles may interfere with good eating habits. Thoughts and feelings can sometimes change food from a friend to an enemy, triggering an eating disorder.

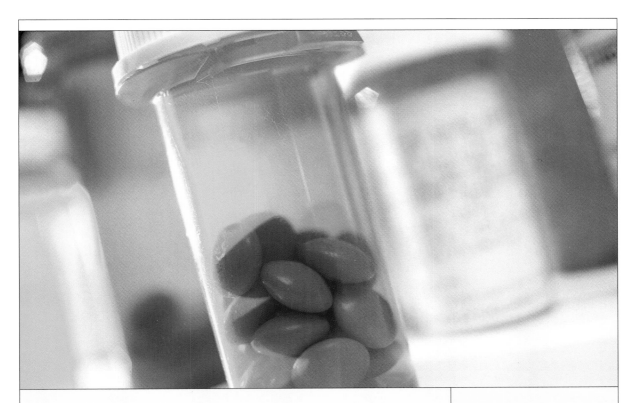

The major eating disorders are anorexia nervosa, bulimia nervosa, and compulsive eating. Other eating disorders include extreme fad dieting and the use of **diet pills**, **laxatives**, and **diuretics** to control weight and body shape.

People with anorexia nervosa, called anorexics, are in a state of self-starvation. People are considered anorexic if they eat little or no food for extended periods of time and their body

Diet pills may help some people lose weight, but they can also contribute to eating disorders.

diet pills: prescription medication used to decrease appetite in order to lose weight

weight drops to less than 85 percent of what is considered normal for their age and height. Anorexia is not a disease that is caught like a cold, and it's not a genetic disorder. Usually, it begins with an intense fear of becoming fat or gaining weight. Anorexics are unable to objec-

laxatives: medicine to loosen the bowels and relieve constipation

Anorexia is a disease that distorts the way people see themselves. Anorexics see food as an enemy, even as they become unhealthily thin.

All people have a unique weight that is right for them, depending on the height and build of their body.

diuretics: anything that increases the amount of urine expelled from the body

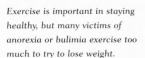

Exercise is important in staying healthy, but many victims of anorexia or bulimia exercise too much to try to lose weight.

tively watch their own weight or body shape. In the battle between brain and body, the anorexic's brain is telling the body lies such as "You're fat," "You're disgusting," or "You're worthless." When a person believes the lies, she is more likely to do things that harm her own health.

Numerous medical problems result from anorexia. Starvation slows the functioning of

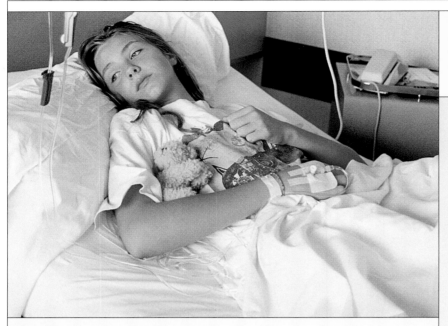

Depriving the body of food can lead to many serious health problems.

thyroid: a gland in the neck that helps to regulate body growth and development

The symptoms of anorexia were first described by physicians more than 300 years ago, making it the first known eating disorder.

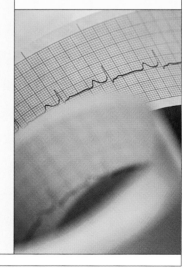

the **thyroid**, as well as breathing, pulse, and blood pressure rates. It dries and yellows the skin and makes bones brittle. Because anorexics have so little body fat, they often develop a fine coat of soft hair called lanugo over their skin to protect them from the cold. Other common problems include **anemia**, swollen joints, reduced muscle mass, lightheadedness, irregular heart rhythms, and shrinking of the brain. In

Anorexia and bulimia can cause life-threatening medical emergencies such as heart attacks.

1998, the American Anorexia/Bulimia Association (AABA) estimated that about one percent of teenage girls in the United States develop anorexia. Approximately one out of every 10 anorexics eventually die from starvation, cardiac arrest, or suicide.

anemia: a condition in which the blood does not have enough red blood cells

MISUSING FOOD

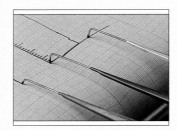

About 50 percent of anorexics also suffer from the second main eating disorder: bulimia nervosa, the practice of binging, or eating large amounts of food, and then quickly getting rid of it. There are two forms of bulimia: purging and nonpurging. Bulimics who purge force themselves to vomit, or they might use

laxatives to get rid of food after an episode of binging. Nonpurging bulimics do not get rid of the food they have eaten, but they may **fast**, go on an extremely strict diet, or exercise uncontrollably after binging in an attempt to burn calories.

Bulimia can cause many medical problems. **Malnutrition**, menstrual irregularity, dry skin, and hair loss can occur. Vomiting brings stomach acids into the mouth, and repeated purging causes sore throats and tooth enamel decay. **Salivary** glands expand, causing the face to swell up. More serious problems can also arise, including irregular heartbeats, muscle weakness, kidney damage, and **epileptic** seizures. Long-term use of laxatives can result in a rupturing of the stomach. In some cases, constant vomiting causes an **electrolytic** imbalance that can bring on heart failure and death. Bulimics can also

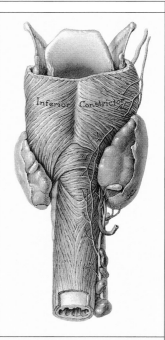

The repeated purging of a bulimic can damage parts of the mouth and throat region.

fast: to stop eating food for an unusually long time

malnutrition: poor health or nutrition caused by an inadequate or unbalanced diet

salivary: relating to saliva, which helps the body to swallow and digest food

Binge eating is often an indication of a psychological disorder such as depression.

rupture their esophagus or choke to death while vomiting.

The third enemy of good nutrition is compulsive eating. This uncontrolled eating may occur regularly or from time to time, secretly or in front of others. Compulsive eating is often a symptom of depression or other psychological problems. Some of the danger signals are episodes of binge eating and the inability to stop eating voluntarily. Compulsive eaters usually overeat even when they are not hungry and gain weight unusually fast.

Bulimia is a sickness that requires counseling or medical attention. Without help, the problem usually only worsens.

cholesterol: a clear substance found in human and animal tissues; too much of it in the body can clog blood vessels

obese: extremely overweight

Health problems caused by compulsive eating include a fast or irregular heart rate, high blood pressure, raised **cholesterol** levels, joint pain, and poor blood circulation. According to the AABA, about 40 percent of **obese** people are compulsive eaters.

In addition to the psychological reasons for eating disorders, biological causes also play a role in some problems. In a small number of cases, obesity or excessive thinness is caused by a malfunctioning thyroid gland. Another physical factor in abnormal weight is **metabolism**.

metabolism: the chemical processes that result in growth and energy in the body

A key step in overcoming any eating disorder is becoming comfortable with your natural body type.

Some overweight people have slower metabolisms, causing their bodies to burn fewer calories per hour than the average person. A faster metabolism may be responsible for someone being unusually thin. But true eating disorders usually stem from the intense desire to change one's body size or image.

MIRROR, MIRROR ON THE WALL

Nearly all victims of eating disorders have low self-esteem. They feel that they are judged by others on their appearance, and that their lives would get better if they lost weight. This type of thinking often leads to an obsessive desire for physical perfection. Usually, the "ideal" goals that people set for themselves are

unhealthy and unattainable. When they push themselves to attain a perfect body, they start to believe that if 100 pounds (45 kg) is a good weight, then 95 (43 kg) will be better. The drive for a perfect body is often shaped by the unrealistic standards set by our **culture**.

Participation in certain athletics can also negatively influence a person's eating habits. The

culture: a society and its combination of knowledge, beliefs, and behaviors

Our culture often portrays thinner as better. This has a major influence on what many people consider the perfect body.

Exercise is good for the body, but too much concern over physical appearances may lead to eating disorders.

emphasis that society, coaches, and parents place on winning may also directly encourage young athletes to strive for ideal body weights and shapes, leading to eating disorders. According to one 1992 study, eating disorders affect more than 60 percent of female athletes in sports such as figure skating and gymnastics. Famous gymnasts Kathy Johnson, Nadia

Comaneci, and Cathy Rigby have all admitted to fighting eating disorders.

Gymnast Christy Henrich didn't live to admit her problem. In her struggle to lower her weight, Christy developed anorexia and bulimia.

At one point, her weight plummeted to 47 pounds (21 kg). In 1994, at the age of 22, Christy died of multiple organ failure.

Competitors may achieve greater athletic success and receive praise from coaches and the media when they maintain a particular body size or shape. But trying too hard to create a different body than the one a person is born with can be frustrating and dangerous.

Good health does not apply just to the body. It also involves having a positive outlook about yourself.

WINNING THE BATTLE

The first step in winning the battle with an eating disorder is admitting that there is a problem. Remaining in denial will only worsen the problem. The second step is getting help immediately. It is important to find someone to talk with, such as a family member, counselor, or doctor.

The third, and most difficult step, is for people to accept who they really are. Getting rid of self-condemning thought patterns is very important. Moving on from past self-doubts will set people free and enable them to look at themselves in the mirror with confidence. Food will no longer be seen as an enemy. It will once again be seen as something to enjoy, something that sustains good health, and something that adds variety to life.

Talking to someone about an eating disorder can make the road to recovery much easier.

OVERCOMING ILLNESS

CATHY RIGBY
WORLD CHAMPION GYMNAST

Cathy Rigby made her musical acting debut in "The Wizard of Oz" in 1981, flying through the air via a tornado in her role as Dorothy. She later flew across the stage as Peter Pan in another theater production. But acting was not Cathy's first great accomplishment. Her first claim to fame was flying high on a balance beam. As a pigtailed 15-year-old, she competed in the 1968 Summer Olympics in Mexico City, achieving the highest U.S. scores in gymnastics. The first American woman to win a medal in the World Gymnastics competition, Cathy earned a total of 12 international medals, eight of them gold.

As the world was applauding her accomplishments, however, Cathy was plagued by a secret that was destroying her. What began as an attempt to lose weight before her second Olympics became an obsession to have a perfect body. In the 12-year battle

with anorexia and bulimia that followed, Cathy was hospitalized twice when her body went into cardiac arrest. "That drive that makes you great at what you do athletically—the willingness to push through the pain, the perfectionist drive—is the same [thing] that pushes you to attain the perfect body any way you can," Cathy later explained.

Now, years after overcoming her illness, Cathy is a popular speaker who spends much of her time discussing the importance of good nutrition and balanced health. She has produced such videos as *Faces of Recovery* and *Cathy Rigby on Eating Disorders*, which provide help for victims of eating disorders and their families.

In September 1997, the NBC television station aired the movie *Perfect Body*, the story of a young gymnast who is willing to lose weight any way she can in order to compete. Cathy was deeply involved in the film, which paralleled her life and provided firsthand information on eating disorders. "What makes this movie different," Cathy said, "is that you really see where the responsibility lies in who is to blame and who is accountable—how the coaches, the parents, and the gymnast herself are responsible."

Cathy's first step in conquering her eating disorder was admitting she had a problem. Twelve years after the illness first affected her, she won her battle with anorexia. "Since 1983," she said proudly, "it doesn't run my life anymore."

American Anorexia/Bulimia Association
165 West 46th Street
Suite 1108
New York, NY 10036   www.aabainc.org

American College of Sports Medicine
c/o Public Information Office
P.O. Box 1440
Indianapolis, IN 46206

Anorexia Nervosa and Related Eating Disorders, Inc.
P.O. Box 5102
Eugene, OR 97405   www.anred.com

Anorexics, Bulimics Anonymous National
Service Office
P.O. Box 47573
Phoenix, AZ 85968

Bulimia/Anorexia Self-Help
Deaconess Hospital
6150 Oakland Avenue
St. Louis, MO 63139

National Anorectic Aid Society
5796 Karl Road
Columbus, OH 43229

National Association of Anorexia Nervosa and
Associated Disorders
P.O. Box 7
Highland Park, IL 60035

Overeaters Anonymous, Inc.
World Service Office
6075 Zenith Court NE
Rio Rancho, NM 87124   www.overeatersanonymous.org